Disney

MINNIE & DAISY

BEST FRIENDS FOREVER

For more information address Disney Press,
114 Fifth Avenue, New York, New York 10011-5690.

ISBN 978-1-4231-7404-2

J689-1817-1-13060
Printed in the United States of America

First Edition

10 9 8 7 6 5 4 3 2 1

Disney

Minnie & Daisy

Best Friends Forever

THE PESKY PET

Disney PRESS
New York

PORT

Chapter 1

"Six in the morning is too early to be awake," somebody moaned. "Why did I sign up for this?"

All the other kids in the surfing class were sleepy. But Daisy was wide awake. She couldn't wait to go surfing for the first time.

Daisy loved sports. She already played tennis, basketball, golf, rugby, squash, baseball . . . and even Ping-Pong.

And she knew she would love surfing!

"Okay!" the instructor said. She put her surfboard down onto the sand.

Premier
Surfing
DAISY

"Before you get in the water, you have to learn how to 'pop up,'" she said.

Daisy watched eagerly. The teacher lay down on her stomach on the board. She placed her hands under her shoulders, as though she were about to do a push-up. Then she leaped up to a crouch. She balanced on the board with her legs wide and her knees bent. She looked as though she were surfing on dry land! Daisy giggled.

"Now you try," the teacher said to her. Daisy copied her motions. "Popping up" was tricky—Daisy almost lost her balance. She put her arms out and pretended she was riding a huge wave.

Soon everyone in the class had learned how to pop up onto the board. Nobody looked sleepy anymore. They couldn't wait to start the real surfing.

"Into the water!" the teacher said. Everyone paddled out into the ocean on their surfboards.

Daisy waited for a wave to reach her. Then she tried to stand up on her board. It was a lot harder than doing it on dry land! The board kept sliding out from under her.

But pretty soon, Daisy had the hang of it. When the next wave reached her, she pushed up off her hands and jumped into a crouch. She was the first person in the class to stand up!

The class was over much too soon. Daisy felt a pang as she paddled her board back to shore. Surfing was amazing! The rush of the waves . . . the wind in her feathers . . . the water swirling around her feet . . . it was like flying. Daisy was in love.

She handed the rented surfboard back to the instructor. "Thanks," Daisy said. "That was amazing."

The teacher smiled and gave Daisy a thumbs-up. "You're a natural, Daisy," she said. "You should keep it up."

"I want to do this all the time," Daisy said. "I need my own surfboard so I can practice every day!"

Chapter 2

"And then, the next wave was even better!" Daisy said. It was Monday morning, and she was telling Minnie about surfing. "And the wave after that—"

"Okay, okay," Minnie said. "I get the point. You're crazy for surfing."

"I wish I could surf every day," Daisy said. "The instructor said that I have a real talent for it! But I really need to get my own board—just like the one I rented for the lesson."

"What does it look like?" Minnie asked.

"It's pink with a purple Hawaiian design," Daisy said. "And it's six feet long. It looks like a giant, beautiful tropical fish."

Minnie looked impressed. "**Awesome.**"

"I'll get a matching swimsuit and I'll practice every morning before school!" Daisy said. She could just see it now. The guys in her surf class would be totally impressed. And so would her teacher!

"**Do you have enough money to buy a surfboard?**" Minnie asked.

Daisy sighed. “No,” she said. “I spent all my birthday money on new tennis outfits.”

“What about your allowance?” Minnie asked. “You could save up for a couple of months.”

“It would take me years to save enough for a board,” Daisy said. “And I always end up spending it on concert tickets and baseball cards, anyway.”

The friends walked together in silence. Daisy thought hard.

“No,” she said finally, “my allowance isn’t enough for a board. I think I need a job.”

“What kind of job?” Minnie said. “Like my job, babysitting?”

"Maybe," Daisy said. "I'm good at lots of stuff. I bet I could get any kind of job I wanted. I could mow people's lawns. I could wash cars. I could give tennis lessons. I could deliver newspapers. And before I know it, I'll have enough money for **Humuhumunukunukuapua'a!**"

"Bless you," Minnie said.

"I didn't sneeze, silly," Daisy said. "That's the name of the Hawaiian state fish. I'm naming my surfboard after it."

"You don't have a surfboard," Minnie said.

Daisy corrected her. "I don't have a surfboard *yet*."

The bell rang. They were late for class!

Chapter 3

Daisy met up with Minnie and their friend Nancy at lunch.

"What's up?" Nancy said.

"I need a job," Daisy said.

"Why?" Nancy asked.

"Humuhumunukunukuapua'a. It will be mine," Daisy said seriously. "I must have it."

"**What?**" Nancy said. She looked completely confused.

"Don't ask," Minnie advised Nancy. "Daisy," Minnie went on, "do you really have time for a job?"

Daisy thought it over. It was true—she did have tennis practice three days a week. And she had a weekly soccer game.

"And you just joined the Junior Billiards Club," Minnie added.

"And you always ride your bike on the boardwalk on Sundays," Nancy said.

"I'll quit billiards," Daisy decided. "And put my bike in the garage."

"Don't forget about homework," Minnie said.

"And the Chickadee Patrol," Nancy reminded her.

"It doesn't matter!" Daisy said impatiently. "I'll find the time. I want that surfboard!"

Nancy looked even more confused.

"Humunuku-thingy is a surfboard?"

Daisy nodded.

"If you get a job," Nancy said, "will you still have time to help me?"

"Help you with what?" Minnie asked.

"Oh, yeah," Daisy said. She had almost forgotten! "I'm helping Nancy out with life science class."

"We have to dissect a worm," Nancy said. "I'm afraid of worms."

"You're afraid of everything, Nancy," Minnie said.

It was true. Nancy had every phobia—heights, water, bugs, snakes, dogs—even paper cuts.

But especially worms.

"I'm going to do all the lab work," Daisy said, "so Nancy doesn't have to touch a worm."

"That's really nice of you, Daisy," Minnie said.

"Well," Daisy said, "I am getting something in return."

"Daisy has a crush on a boy in my band class," Nancy said.

"He plays the drums," Daisy said. The thought of him made her heart beat faster—just like a drum!

"I'm going to find out his name and see if he likes Daisy back," Nancy explained to Minnie.

"I see," Minnie said to Nancy. "So you're playing Cupid for Daisy to get out of having to touch a worm."

"Yep!" Nancy replied.

"That's it!" Daisy cried. She couldn't believe she hadn't thought of it before.

"What's 'it'?" Minnie asked. "Did you think of a job you can do?"

"I can be a matchmaker!" Daisy said. "Just like Nancy! I'll help other students get to know each other and go out on dates. I'll write love letters for them. I'll help them do their hair! And I'll make millions!"

Minnie and Nancy looked at each other.

"Daisy," Minnie said gently, "someone who *needs* a matchmaker probably shouldn't try to *be* a matchmaker."

Chapter 4

Daisy realized that her BFF was right.

"Okay," Daisy said, "so maybe I'm not meant to be a matchmaker. But I still need to get a job. Today, after school, I'll start looking. And I'm going to take the first job I can find."

"Except if it has to do with romance, right?" Nancy said.

Daisy sighed. "Right," she agreed.

On the way home from school, Daisy decided to stop at her neighbor's house.

"Mr. Marmot's yard is always overgrown,"

Daisy said to herself. "I bet he'd love to hire me to mow it."

Sure enough, the lawn was covered in dandelions and other weeds. The cracks in the sidewalk had trees sprouting in them. And the garden was in need of some **real help.**

"This is perfect," Daisy said happily. She marched up the walk and rang Mr. Marmot's doorbell.

The door opened, and Mr. Marmot peered out at Daisy.

"Hi!" Daisy said. "I need a job. Can I mow your lawn?"

"Sure," Mr. Marmot said. "What do you charge?"

"I have no idea," Daisy admitted.

"How about twenty-five dollars?" Mr. Marmot said.

"It's a deal!" Daisy said. She shook his hand. Twenty-five dollars! That was more than she expected.

Daisy got to work. First she mowed the lawn. But it didn't take very long. And twenty-five dollars was a lot of money. Daisy wanted to do a really good job. So she trimmed the hedges. Then she swept the front walk, watered the flowers, and scrubbed the lawn gnome.

Soon, Daisy had run out of things to do. She put the watering can back in the shed. And that's when she saw them.

Weeds.

Mr. Marmot's flower bed was full of them! Little, scraggly plants with no blossoms on them.

Daisy grabbed a trowel and got to work digging up the weeds. It was hard work. And she was careful to leave the actual flowers alone.

"Mr. Marmot isn't going to believe his eyes!" Daisy said to herself as she weeded. "Lawn mowed. Hedges trimmed. Walk swept. Flowers watered. Gnome bathed. And flower bed weeded! He'll want me to come back every week!"

Daisy dug and dug. She pulled up every weed she could find. Soon she was covered in bits of leaves and smears of dirt. But then . . .

"My prize bog lilies!" Mr. Marmot exclaimed

behind her. Daisy whirled around.

"What? Where?" she asked. She had a bad feeling she knew the answer.

"There!" Mr. Marmot said. He pointed to the pile of "weeds" she had pulled up.

"**Uh-oh,**" Daisy said. This was bad.

"Take your twenty-five dollars and never come back!" Mr. Marmot said. His face was red.

"I'm so sorry!" Daisy said. "Please, keep the money."

Chapter 5

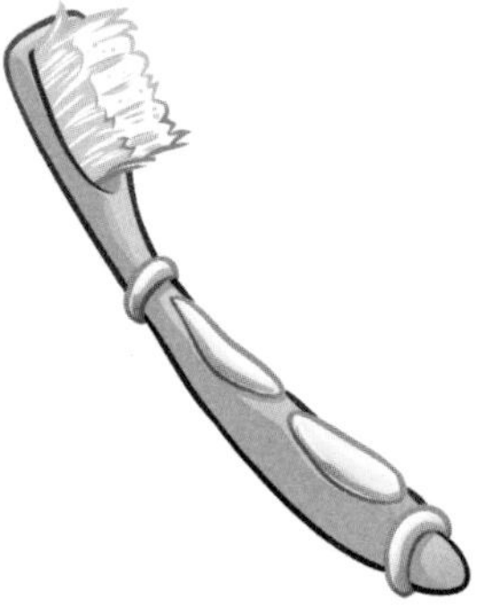

Daisy walked home feeling terrible. She had screwed up. Mr. Marmot might never forgive her. **And she was still broke.**

But she wasn't going to stop looking for work. She would find a job if it was the last thing she did. Her future as a famous surfer depended on it!

That night as she brushed her teeth and got ready for bed, Daisy made a plan.

In the morning, Daisy skipped breakfast and went straight to the copy shop. She typed up an advertisement on the computer there. Daisy listed every kind of job she thought she could do.

She thought about adding matchmaking to the list. But she knew Minnie and Nancy would see it. And they were probably right. Daisy could barely handle her own love life. She wouldn't be able to help someone else with theirs.

Soon Daisy was done. She printed out one hundred copies of the flyer.

"Perfect," she said. **She'd get a job for sure!**

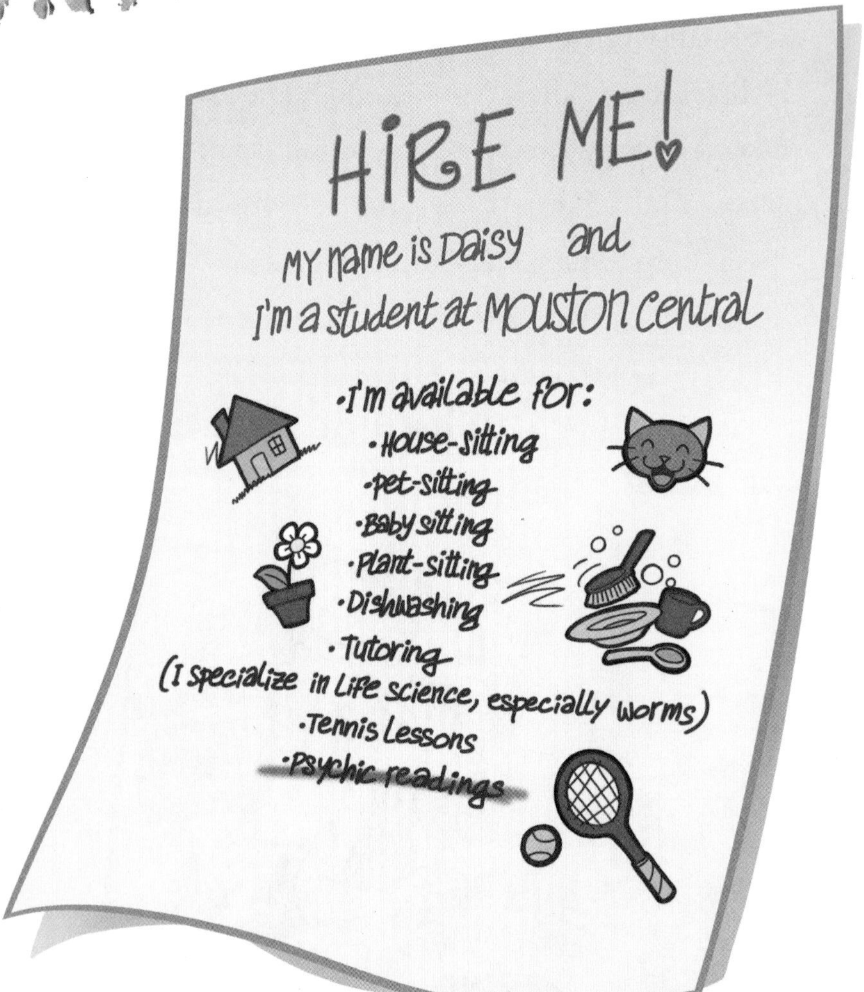

HIRE ME!
MY name is Daisy and
I'm a student at MOUSTON central
•I'm available for:
•House-sitting
•pet-sitting
•Baby sitting
•Plant-sitting
•Dishwashing
•Tutoring
(I specialize in Life science, especially worms)
•Tennis Lessons
•Psychic readings

Daisy practically ran out of the copy shop. She couldn't wait to start putting the ads up!

"**Hey, BFF!**"

Daisy turned around at the sound of Minnie's voice.

"Minnie!" she said. "Look what I made!"

Minnie read the ad Daisy gave her. "It's great," she said. "But . . . are you really qualified for all of these jobs?"

Daisy felt a little hurt. "What do you mean?"

"Psychic readings?" Minnie said. "Really?"

"How hard can it be?" Daisy asked. "I'm totally sensitive to energies. The school nurse said so."

"She said **you're sensitive to allergies,**" Minnie replied.

"Oops," Daisy said. So much for psychic readings.

Chapter 6

Daisy and Minnie spent the morning passing out the ads. They put flyers under people's doors. They put them in mailboxes. They pinned some to the bulletin board at the market. Daisy even put one in the cafeteria at Glomgold Preparatory School—Mouston's biggest rival.

The last stop was the ice cream parlor. Daisy hung her last flyer in the window.

"**Good luck!**" Minnie said. "See you later! I'm off to my piano lesson."

Daisy went home. All she had to do now was

wait. Soon the phone would start ringing. She **knew it!**

While she waited, Daisy played "Duck Duck Dance Battle," her favorite video game. She spun and jumped and shimmied and sashayed. She got a top score on "Shake a Tail Feather."

The phone rang.

"Duck Enterprises," Daisy said into the phone. "No job too small! This is Daisy speaking."

"Hi, Daisy," said a woman's voice. "This is Lucinda Labrador. I found your flyer at Starducks coffee shop."

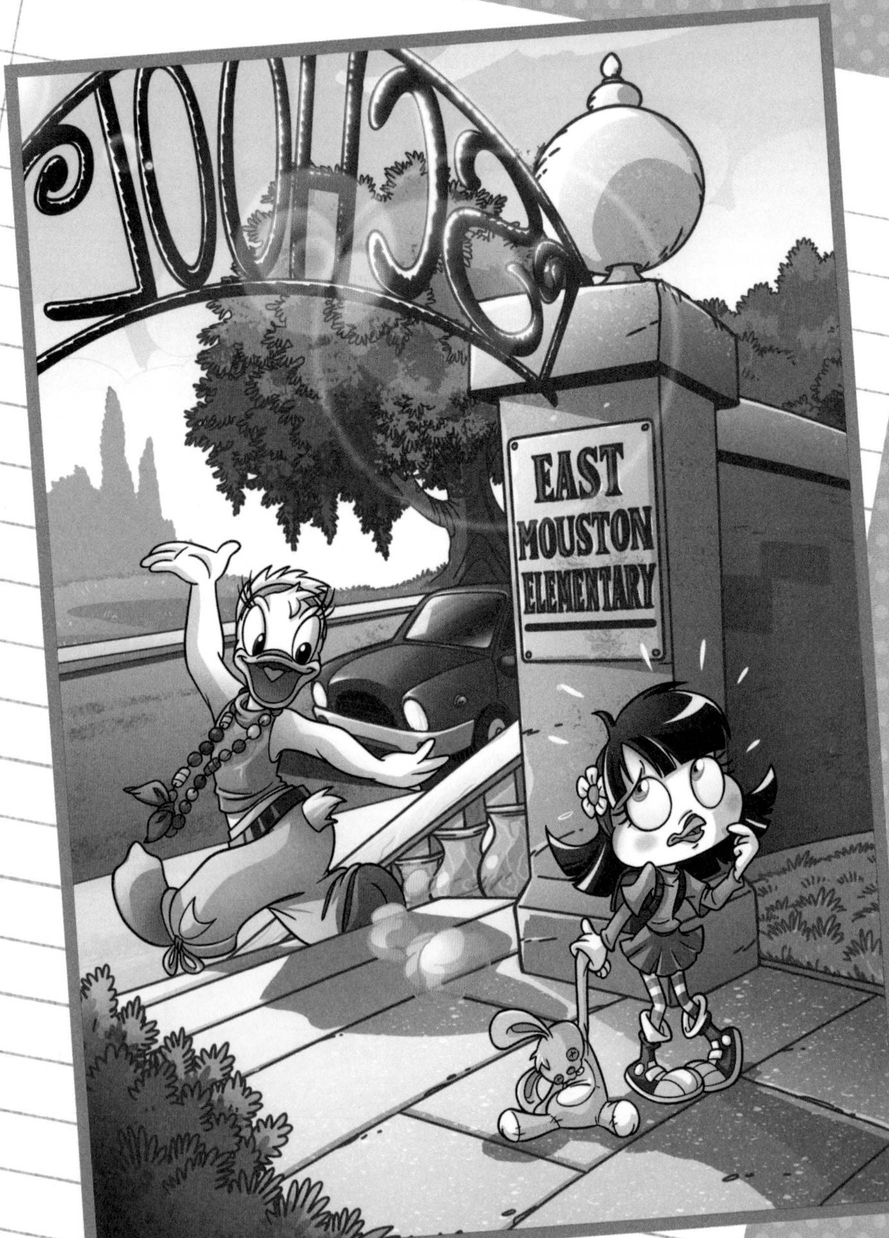
SCHOOL
EAST
MOUSTON
ELEMENTARY

Daisy knew Ms. Labrador. She owned the Mouston movie theater.

"**I have a job for you,**" Ms. Labrador said. "There's a film festival on Monday at my theater. It starts early, and I have to be there. I need you to walk my daughter to school. She's six."

"I'd be delighted," Daisy said in a professional voice. She hung up the phone, and then she did a crazy victory dance. Everything was working out! This would be so easy.

And it *was* easy. Daisy walked little Annabelle Labrador to East Mouston Elementary in the morning. Then she went on to her own school.

But that afternoon, the phone rang again.

"Daisy," Ms. Labrador said, "I went to West Mouston Elementary this afternoon to pick up my daughter. She wasn't there."

"**Uh-oh,**" Daisy said. She had taken Annabelle to the wrong school! So much for easy.

Luckily, Annabelle was fine—just confused. But Daisy knew Ms. Labrador wouldn't be calling again.

Daisy wasn't too worried, though. The phone kept ringing.

First, she got a job washing dishes for Mr. Skink's birthday party. It was going great until . . .

"Wak!" Daisy yelled as she tripped over the Skinks' pet dog, Atilla. She staggered, trying to keep her balance. But then she slipped in a puddle of dishwater. The stack of clean plates went flying. **Crash!**

"Oops," Daisy said. So much for washing dishes.

Daisy's next job was teaching her friend Leonard to play tennis.

"So," Daisy said to Leonard after their first lesson, "I always thought you liked video games better than sports."

"I do," Leonard said. "And I just got the Roger Featherer edition of 'Super Smash Tennis' for my QuackBox 480."

"What's QuackBox 480?" Daisy asked.

"It's the newest and coolest gaming system, of course!" Leonard answered. "They took the QuackBox 320 and added a camera that senses your body movements. So I had to learn the basics of tennis in order to serve and volley correctly. But I think I know enough now to beat the next level against Andy Rodduck. Thanks."

"**Oooookay,**" Daisy said. So much for teaching tennis.

The next week, Daisy accidentally set off the fire alarm at Dr. Snowshoe's house. So much for house-sitting.

"The capital of New York State is New York City," Daisy said. She was tutoring the foreign-exchange student, Gretel.

"No, it is not," Gretel said. "The capital of New York State is Albany, population ninety-eight thousand."

So much for tutoring.

"Aaaahhh-choo!"

So much for plant-sitting.

Chapter 7

Daisy was fed up.

"I've had nine jobs in ten days," she said to Minnie on the phone. "And they were all disasters!"

"Maybe you need a break," Minnie said. "You could try working for yourself for a little while. You could make something and sell it."

"Like a good old-fashioned lemonade stand!" Daisy said. She loved the idea.

"Yeah!" Minnie said. "And we can bake

chocolate chip cookies and sell those with the lemonade!"

"Come over," Daisy said, "and let's do this!"

Ten minutes later, Minnie and Daisy were in Daisy's kitchen reading Agatha Anteater's *Baking for Beginners*.

"Frozen lemonade concentrate," Daisy read from the lemonade recipe.

"Four cups flour," Minnie read from the chocolate chip cookie recipe.

"We need to go to the grocery store," Daisy said. Her pantry was almost empty.

Daisy and Minnie pulled their bikes up at the store.

"Hey," Minnie said, "I have an idea. What if this isn't just a lame old lemonade stand? What if it's a gourmet lemonade stand? With organic everything?"

"Uh—" Daisy started. But Minnie interrupted her.

"Forget the lemonade concentrate. We're making it from scratch! And we should make pink lemonade! With strawberry juice! It's so much prettier! And the cookies should have Belgian chocolate in them."

"I guess?" Daisy said.

"This is going to be perfect!" Minnie said. She pulled Daisy into the store.

"Where is the organic, fair-trade brown sugar?" Minnie muttered. She glared at the shelves in the grocery store. "And I can't believe they only have Swiss chocolate, not Belgian. What is up with that?"

"Maybe we can use regular sugar," Daisy suggested.

"No!" Minnie snapped. Daisy jumped. Minnie wasn't usually this stubborn. But it was actually sort of fun to see her all fired up. Daisy was always the one in charge of their adventures. Watching Minnie take charge was entertaining.

Finally, they found the right kind of sugar. And the organic lemons. And spelt flour for the cookies.

"What's spelt?" Daisy said.

"I have no idea," Minnie admitted. "But it's supposed to be really good for you."

Back at Daisy's house, Minnie and Daisy got to work. They squeezed the lemons. Then they squeezed the strawberries. Or they tried to, anyway.

"**My shirt!**" Daisy said. She was covered in strawberry juice.

"Sorry!" Minnie said. She pulled half a strawberry out of her ear.

Finally, the lemonade was done. And the organic, vegan, gluten-free cookies were out of the oven.

"Now all we have to do is set up a table on the street," Daisy said.

"Um, Daisy?" Minnie said, looking out the window. "What time is it?"

Daisy checked her phone. "**Oh no!**" she moaned. "It's after nine o'clock! No one wants to buy lemonade at night!"

Minnie poured Daisy a glass of lemonade and helped herself to a cookie.

"What a disaster," Daisy said.

"I'm sorry—this is all my fault," Minnie said.

"No, not the lemonade stand," Daisy said. "The whole job thing. I keep getting fired. Or quitting. I can't even employ myself."

"**Don't blame yourself.** You just haven't found the right job," Minnie said. "You're the smartest, stubbornest person I know. You'll figure something out."

"Sure," Daisy said. She liked hearing Minnie say those nice things about her. She just wasn't sure she believed them.

Chapter 8

The next day at school, Daisy was getting ready for tennis practice when Minnie came running down the hall.

"Daisy!" she said. "Do you have plans for this afternoon? Because I think I found a job for you!"

"Awesome!" Daisy said. She hugged Minnie. It was good to have a BFF watching out for you. "What is it?"

"**Babysitting with me!**" Minnie said with a huge grin.

MOUSTON
TENNIS
TEAM

"You know how I babysit for Lilac Shetland?" Minnie said. Daisy nodded. "Well," Minnie went on, "Mrs. Shetland just had a new baby. And I can't keep up with Lilac and take care of little Lyle. So I asked Mrs. Shetland if you could be my partner!"

"**Perfect!**" Daisy said.

"They're little angels," Minnie said. "They won't give us any trouble. This is going to be so much fun! I can't wait to work with my BFF!"

"Right back atcha!" Daisy said.

So after tennis practice, Daisy met Minnie in front of the school. They walked to the Shetlands' house.

"Today I'm just going to introduce you," Minnie said. "Mrs. Shetland said you could start tomorrow, if the interview goes well."

Daisy gulped. "**Interview?**"

"Don't worry," Minnie said. "She's really nice. I'm sure the interview will be a piece of cake."

"Organic, fair-trade cake?" Daisy said. She poked Minnie in the side. Minnie laughed.

"Yep," she said. "Gluten-free vegan cake."

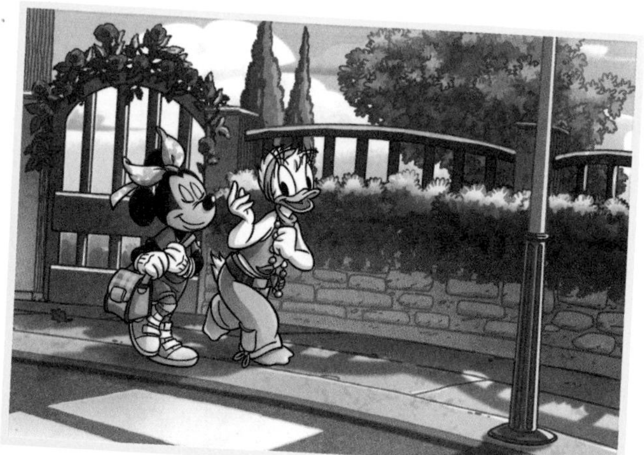

Chapter 9

"So, Daisy," Mrs. Shetland said, "have you ever babysat before?"

"Sort of!" Daisy said. She was about to tell Mrs. Shetland about walking Annabelle to school. But then she remembered how that had ended. She didn't want Mrs. Shetland to know about little Annabelle Labrador's single day as a student at East Mouston Elementary.

"Actually, not really," Daisy said. "No. I haven't babysat before. **At all. Ever.**" Technically, walking Annabelle to school wasn't

babysitting. It was more like chaperoning. Or something. Anyway, Daisy was pretty sure she wasn't lying. Not technically.

"Have you ever had a job before?" Mrs. Shetland asked.

"Yes," Daisy said. "Lots of jobs, actually."

That was true enough!

"Well," Mrs. Shetland said, "Minnie is an expert. I trust her judgment. She says you are responsible enough to take care of my children. So, welcome aboard! You can start tomorrow."

The next day, Daisy arrived at the Shetlands' house right on time. Minnie was already there. She looked frazzled.

"Here," Minnie said, handing the baby to Daisy. "Can you take Lyle for a second? Lilac just threw her sandwich into the fish bowl."

"Eep," Daisy said, as Minnie pushed the baby into her arms. Daisy nearly dropped the squirming little bundle. She looked down into Lyle's face.

"Hi there, Lyle," Daisy said.

Lyle threw up on her.

"**Minnieeeeee!**" Daisy yelled in a panic.

"What?" Minnie said. "What happened?"

"The baby threw up on me," Daisy shrieked. Ugh! This was so gross!

Minnie rolled her eyes. "Babies do that," she said. "There are wipes in the nursery. You can clean him up there."

"What about me?" Daisy said. She showed Minnie her stained shirt.

"It's just a little puke," Minnie said impatiently. "Deal with it." She went back to fishing Lilac's sandwich out of the bowl.

Daisy had never seen this side of Minnie before! Usually Minnie was the delicate one—not Daisy. And usually Minnie was more patient! Daisy remembered how pushy Minnie had been about the lemonade and cookies. This was just like that.

The day only got worse. Lyle threw up again. Lilac tried to flush one of her shoes down the toilet. Then she had a temper tantrum.

All afternoon, Minnie was a whirlwind of motion. She washed jam off Lilac's face and picked crayons up off the carpet. She fed Lyle a bottle and put him down for a nap.

Daisy was amazed at her friend. Babysitting was hard! It was all Daisy could do to keep up with Minnie.

Lyle had only been in his crib for ten minutes when . . .

"**Waaaaahhh!**"

"I thought he was supposed to be asleep!" Daisy said. Minnie sighed. She was making Lilac dinner.

"He probably needs his diaper changed," Minnie said. "**Can you do it?**"

Daisy squared her jaw. She summoned her courage and marched into the nursery. She put Lyle on the changing table. She took a deep breath.

She changed Lyle's diaper. And it was awful.

Moving fast, holding her breath, Daisy did it just like Minnie had taught her. Then she put Lyle in his crib and went back to the kitchen. She had made a decision.

"Minnie," Daisy said, "that was the single grossest thing I have ever done. It was worse than dissecting worms for Nancy. It was worse than the carton of yogurt we found in the back of the fridge that one time."

"The carton of yogurt that expired four years ago?" Minnie said. "The one that grew hair?"

"Yes," Daisy said. "That one. This was worse. The truth is, I'm not babysitting material. I'm sorry."

She steeled herself.

"Minnie, I quit."

Minnie was understanding, thank goodness.

Chapter 10

The next day at school, Daisy was feeling very sorry for herself.

"I just want to surf," Daisy said to Nancy and Minnie. "I've tried every way of earning money, but I keep making a mess of things. And now I've run out of options."

No job meant no surfboard.

Humuhumunukunukuapua'a would never be hers at this rate.

The three friends walked down the hall. Daisy and Nancy were on their way to life sciences.

Minnie had art class during that period.

"I'm sure something will work out," Nancy said. "Or maybe your aunt will forget that your birthday already happened and send you more birthday money. Or maybe you'll win the lottery. Or maybe you'll find some money. Under a rock, maybe. Like buried treasure!"

Minnie didn't say anything.

Daisy was about to ask her what she thought. But then she noticed something. A flyer. It was on the bulletin board outside the teachers' lounge.

"Pet sitter needed!" Daisy read. "You guys, this is my last chance!" Daisy couldn't believe her good luck.

"Perfect!" Nancy said. "**It's fate!**"

Minnie didn't say anything.

The flyer was for Mrs. Flamingo, the art teacher. She needed a pet sitter for the coming weekend, and she was offering to pay seventy-five dollars!

Daisy thought about it. "I already have some money saved up from my other jobs," she said.

She added the numbers quickly in her mind. The dishwashing, plus the house-sitting, plus the tennis lesson, plus the tutoring . . . Yes! If she took the pet-sitting job, she could have enough money **for a new surfboard by Monday!**

Chapter 11

"Everything is finally going to work out!" Daisy said to Nancy and Minnie. "Soon I'll have Humuhumunukunukuapua'a!"

Daisy started to daydream. "I'll practice surfing every day," she said, getting carried away. "I'll get really, really good! I'll win contests! When I grow up, I'll be a professional surfer! I'll star in movies about surfing! I'll have a dolphin friend! And it will all be because of Mrs. Flamingo and her pet!"

"Daisy," Minnie said. The sound of her voice popped Daisy's daydream bubble. "**Are you sure this is a good idea?**"

Daisy felt a pang of hurt. "Why wouldn't it be?" she asked.

"Well," Minnie said, "you've never had a pet. Not even a goldfish."

"So?" Daisy said. She was starting to feel a little annoyed with Minnie. Didn't Minnie believe in her? She had said she did. But had she meant it?

"**You didn't like babysitting,**" Minnie pointed out. "And you have no experience with pets. Can you really take care of a pet by yourself?"

"Bah!" Daisy said. She wasn't going to let Minnie psych her out. She was making a mountain out of a molehill. "Remember the sea monkeys?"

"Ugh!" Nancy squeaked. "I was so scared of them!"

"You know, they're not really sea monkeys," Daisy said. "They're brine shrimp."

"Shrimp," Nancy said. She shuddered. "That's even worse!"

"Anyway, I raised those shrimp for science class," Daisy said. "How much harder could a regular pet be?"

"Sure," Minnie said sarcastically. "And remember how they all died when you forgot to feed them for a couple of days?"

That was enough.

"Minnie," Daisy said, "what is your problem?"

Minnie looked surprised. "What are you talking about?" she said.

"**You want me to fail!**" Daisy said. "A real best friend would back me up!"

"Yeah? Well, a real best friend wouldn't quit a babysitting job in the middle of it," Minnie said. She looked mad, too.

"**You said you didn't mind!**" Daisy shouted at her.

"Well, I lied, Daisy!" Minnie yelled. "And I also lied when I said it wasn't your fault you can't keep a job!"

Chapter 12

Daisy didn't talk to Minnie for the rest of the day.

It was hard to pay attention in class. All Daisy could think about was how angry she was. Minnie was such a . . . a jerk! She knew how hard Daisy had been working. And she had thrown it back in her face.

Daisy was so upset, she was shaking. Her heart was beating a mile a minute. She hated feeling this way. She would never forgive Minnie.

Daisy and Minnie usually sat next to each

other in math class. Today, Daisy couldn't stand the idea of being anywhere near Minnie.

She looked around for another desk. But the only place to sit was her usual spot. Daisy sat down and turned away from Minnie.

"**Psst.**" Minnie poked Daisy. Daisy didn't turn around. She pretended she hadn't noticed.

Neither of the best friends could concentrate during math class. Daisy looked at her math work sheet, but the numbers all ran together.

English class was next.

"Okay, kids, pair up. You're going to be

reading with a buddy today," the teacher said.

"**Daisy,**" Minnie said. Daisy didn't look at her. "**Hey, Daisy!** Will you be my partner?"

Daisy didn't say anything to Minnie. She turned to Leonard. "Let's be partners, Leonard," she said.

"Uh," Leonard said. He looked at Minnie nervously. "Okay—I guess?"

Minnie sighed and paired off with Nancy.

Leonard and Daisy read *A Midsummer Night's Dream* together. But Daisy could barely keep track of her lines. She was so focused on ignoring Minnie that she couldn't think of anything *but* Minnie.

Daisy had a tennis match after school. She tried to put everything out of her mind.

"Just tennis," Daisy said to herself over and over again. "Just tennis."

She won, but just barely. Daisy usually played better. As she left the court, Minnie appeared out of nowhere.

"Hey, nice game!" Minnie said. She had a hopeful smile on her face. Daisy wanted to throw her racket at Minnie's head. She ignored her instead.

Minnie held her hand up for a high five. Daisy walked by her. She looked straight ahead. Her hands stayed clenched around her tennis racket.

Minnie had betrayed her. **She was the worst best friend ever.** She did not deserve a high five.

Chapter 13

That night, Daisy was in the kitchen when the phone rang. She knew it was Minnie. So she let the answering machine pick up.

"Hey, Daisy, it's Minnie. Your BFF." Minnie's voice came out of the machine. "At least I think I'm still your BFF. But that's why I'm calling, I guess. I'm really sorry about—"

Daisy picked up the phone.

"— about today," Minnie said. "Hello? Daisy, are you there?"

"Yeah," Daisy said. She took a deep breath.

"I am so mad at you, Minnie!" she yelled. "You are the absolute worst!"

"Daisy, I—" Minnie started. But Daisy interrupted her.

"Just talking about this makes me so mad I could spit!" Daisy said. "You think you're so perfect, with your fancy little babysitting job! Just because you can change a dirty diaper without wanting to throw up? And then you were so bossy! You're not my boss!"

"Daisy, I'm so sorry—" Minnie tried again.

"I'm totally freaked out, Minnie!" Daisy said. "This job thing has been such a disaster! I thought I'd be able to handle it, no problem. I mean, I'm smart, right? I'm responsible! I'm good at stuff!

So why can't I get this right?"

Suddenly, Daisy wasn't even mad anymore. She was just sad.

"And then you were so mean to me." Her

voice cracked. Daisy hated crying. She wasn't going to cry. She wasn't.

There was a silence. And then Minnie said, "Okay. Just because you aren't good at something right away doesn't mean you shouldn't keep trying, right?"

Daisy sniffled. "Right."

"So you're going to keep trying. And I will help you. And I will quit being so bossy."

Chapter 14

Now that she had patched things up with Minnie, Daisy was feeling much better.

Saturday morning had arrived, and Daisy stood on Mrs. Flamingo's front step. She hopped up and down in place. She was trying to psych herself up, like she did before a soccer match.

"You'll be fine," she told herself. "How hard could it be to take care of a fish or a gerbil?"

Mrs. Flamingo welcomed Daisy into her living room. She disappeared for a minute and returned holding a small, gray, googly-eyed, rat-squirrel-alien thingy.

"What is that?" Daisy squeaked.

Mrs. Flamingo smiled fondly at the gerbil-sized creature. It made a high-pitched chittering noise. Daisy jumped.

"This is Sugarplum," Mrs. Flamingo said. "He is a sugar glider."

"Ah, yes," Daisy said. She nodded wisely. "A sugar glider."

Minnie better have meant it when she said she'd help me, Daisy thought. I think I'm going to need it. **What the heck is a sugar glider?!**

"No chocolate, no coffee, no wheat, no beans, no soda, no juice, no peanuts—he's allergic—no loud noises, no late nights, no sudden movements . . ."

Mrs. Flamingo was going over her instruction sheet with Daisy.

". . . **no pop** music, and **absolutely no sugar.** It makes him uncontrollably hyper!" she finished. "But other than that, you can do whatever you want!"

Daisy nodded. **I can do this, she told herself.**

Daisy felt surprisingly calm.

This job will not be a disaster, she thought, trying to keep a positive attitude.

Plus, she always had her friends to rely on. Minnie would help her—hopefully without getting **too bossy!** And Leonard and Nancy were going to help, as well. Leonard had even installed a Pet Facts app on Daisy's Flipazoid.

Daisy would be fine. She knew it. Maybe.

Chapter 15

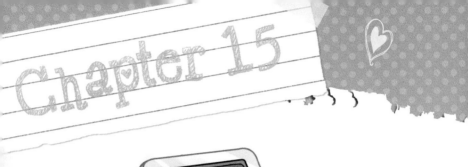

"That's it!" Mrs. Flamingo said. "I'm off!"

"Bye," Daisy said. "I promise to take good care of Sugarplum."

"Good," Mrs. Flamingo said. "He's my little angel. Don't let anything happen to him."

Mrs. Flamingo shut the door behind her. Daisy looked at the "little angel," and it looked back at her.

There was a wicked twinkle in its angelic little eye.

"Well, Sugarplum," Daisy said. "It's just

BFF

you and me now." She put her finger up so Sugarplum could sniff it. But the creature leaped away! It dived under a cabinet and hid.

"Great," Daisy said. "Okay, time for Leonard's pet encyclopedia." She started up the Pet Facts app. But . . .

"**Hurgeborg da flommerbot?**" Daisy read aloud. "What language is this in?"

It certainly wasn't in English. She browsed through a few other sections of the program. Everything was in the same mystery language.

"**Argh!**" Daisy said. "Thanks a lot, Leonard!"

Chapter 16

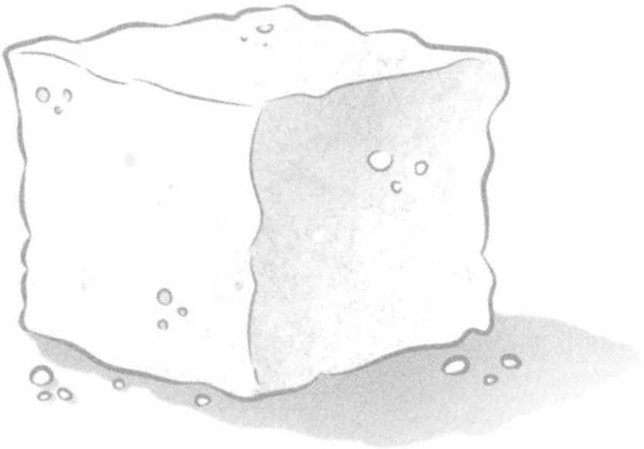

"Heeere, glider glider glider," Daisy crooned.

She waved a sugar cube near where Sugarplum was hiding. "You like sugar, don't you?" she said. "Come and get it!"

Sugarplum's nose appeared first, nostrils twitching. The second he was out from under the cabinet, Daisy pounced.

"Aha!" she cried. She scooped Sugarplum up in his carrier and shut the door.

"I'm a genius," Daisy said. "This is going to be—"

SWEET!

"Eeeeeeeeeeeeeeeeeeeeeee!"

Daisy jumped a mile. What a terrible noise! And it was coming . . . from the carrier. She peered into it.

Sugarplum was having a sugar-glider temper tantrum. He sat in the carrier and glared at Daisy. And the noise didn't stop. It just got louder.

How does such a tiny critter make such a loud noise? Daisy wondered. It sounded like a fire alarm.

Daisy tried giving Sugarplum a snack. He didn't eat it. She tried singing him a song.

He only screeched louder. She tried reasoning with him. She tried yelling at him. She left the room for five minutes.

But she didn't let him out of the carrier. He would just hide again, she was sure of it.

Finally, Daisy gave up. She called Minnie.

"I could use a hand," Daisy said. "Actually, I could use a small army. But you'll have to do."

"That bad, huh?" Minnie said. She sounded kind of amused. "What is it, a guinea pig? No, you sound really freaked out. I bet it's a bunny!"

"Ha-ha," Daisy said, rolling her eyes. "You laugh now, but wait until you see what this thing looks like."

"Well, is it little?" Minnie asked. "You could bring it over. Maybe a change of scene will calm it down."

"Thank you," Daisy said. "We'll be right over. And Minnie?"

"Yes?"

"**Brace yourself.**"

Chapter 17

Daisy put Sugarplum's carrier into her bicycle basket.

She climbed onto her bike and started riding toward Minnie's house. It was a terrifying ride. Sugarplum was still screaming at the top of his lungs. It made it hard for Daisy to concentrate on the road. She veered onto the sidewalk, then back into the street. Sugarplum howled.

Luckily, people could hear her coming a mile away, and stayed out of her way.

gotta talk!

Finally, they got to Minnie's house. Daisy hurried up the stairs with Sugarplum's carrier.

"Eeeeeeeeeeeeeeeeee!" Sugarplum screeched.

"**What on earth is that?!**" Minnie said. She had to shout so Daisy could hear her over the noise.

"This," Daisy said, "is a sugar glider."

"That," Minnie said, "is a very unhappy sugar glider." She paused.

"What's a sugar glider?" Minnie asked.

Daisy told her what Mrs. Flamingo had said—that sugar gliders are like flying squirrels and can make excellent pets.

"Does Mrs. Flamingo keep it in this carrier all the time?" Minnie asked.

"No," Daisy admitted. "But I'm worried if I let him out, he'll hide. And I might never find him."

"You can't really keep him in there for the whole weekend," Minnie said. She had a point.

Daisy looked around Minnie's room—which,

unlike Daisy's room, was neat and organized. "I guess we can let him out in here," she said. "Just as long as we keep the door closed."

Feeling pretty nervous about it, Daisy opened the carrier.

Sugarplum's screeching stopped right away. He walked out of the cage. Daisy and Minnie watched as he climbed onto Minnie's chair. He circled around on the cushion a few times, and then . . .

"**He's going to sleep!**" Daisy said.

"What a relief!"

"While he's sleeping," Minnie said, "let's see what we can find about sugar gliders on the Internet."

There was a lot of information about sugar gliders on the Internet.

"Should we start with WeLoveSugarGliders.com or SugarGliders4Ever.org?" Minnie said.

"Why do people like these things?" Daisy asked. "They look weird, they hide, they cry . . ."

"Okay," Minnie said, "How about ILostMySugarGlider.net/PleaseHelpMeFindIt.php?"

"That sounds about right," Daisy said. "In case he hides again."

"'Question one,'" Minnie read, "'do you know where your sugar glider is?'"

"Duh," Daisy said. "He's right—" she stopped short, staring at the empty chair.

Sugarplum was gone.

"**Uh,**" Daisy said. She looked around Minnie's room. There was no sign of Sugarplum. "Minnie, remember how you insisted that we couldn't keep Sugarplum in his carrier for the entire weekend?"

"Yeah," Minnie said. She was still staring at the computer screen.

"Well," Daisy said, **"I'm not sure that I should have listened to you."**

Chapter 18

Sugarplum was nowhere to be found. He was not under Minnie's bed. He wasn't in it, either.

He wasn't behind her desk, in her garbage can, or on top of her bookcase.

Sugarplum had vanished.

"Sugarplum!" Daisy called. "Please come out, Sugarplum!"

Daisy was starting to panic.

Then Minnie realized that the door of her wardrobe was open. "He must be hiding in there!" she said.

Minnie was right.

Sugarplum was happily chomping away at the neckline of Minnie's fanciest dress.

Minnie was furious.

"That was a Vivienne Mousewood design!" she shouted. "I saved my allowance for six months to buy it on DownByTheBay! And now **it's ruined!"**

Daisy tried to calm her down. "Don't worry," she said. "We both know how good you are with a needle and thread. You'll have it fixed in no time!"

"What if Sugarplum decides to make a snack out of my Jimmy Chews?" Minnie demanded. "You have to get him out of here, now!"

"But where will I take him?" Daisy asked. "**I'm desperate!** And Leonard's animal facts app was no use at all!"

Minnie shook her head. "I have no idea," she said. "But you know who might be able to help? **Nancy!**"

Chapter 19

It was a good idea, actually. Nancy was famous for solving people's problems.

Minnie called Nancy, and they agreed to meet at the ice cream parlor.

"How are we going to get there with . . . that?" Minnie asked. She pointed at Sugarplum's carrier.

"Oh," Daisy said. "It should be okay. I brought him over here on my bike. It was a little scary, but he's stopped screaming. It should be easy as pie this time."

"**Easy as pie, huh?**" Minnie said.

Daisy almost rode her bike into a mailbox.

Sugarplum hadn't started screeching again. But now he was doing something worse. He was so excited to be outside that he was throwing himself from one side of the carrier to the other. Every time he moved, **Daisy's bike almost tipped over.**

"Sure." Daisy panted. She swerved back onto the road. "Easy as fair-trade vegan pie with a gluten-free crust."

SUGAR
MILK

SUGAR

Finally, Daisy and Minnie staggered into the ice cream parlor. They waved at Nancy.

"**What. Is. That?**" said a nasty voice.

Daisy braced herself. It was Abigail, the meanest, most popular girl in school. She was eating ice cream with her minions, Molly and Millie. Gretel, the foreign exchange student, was there, too. Great, Daisy thought, an audience.

"This is Sugarplum," Daisy said. "Mrs. Flamingo's pet. I'm pet-sitting him."

"It looks like an evil scientist crossed a monkey and a rat," Abigail said.

"Get lost, Abigail," Nancy said. "Nobody asked your opinion."

Daisy smiled at Nancy. She was helping already!

"I can't wait to meet the little fella!" Nancy said to Daisy. "I just know we're going to be pals!"

She leaned down and looked into the carrier. "**Get it away! Get it away!**" Nancy shrieked. "It's horrible! An evil scientist must have created it by crossing a monkey and a rat!"

Daisy sighed. Sure, Nancy was afraid of everything. She knew this already. But this was ridiculous.

"It's just a little sugar glider," Daisy said in a coaxing voice. "Come on, Nancy. Come make friends!"

Chapter 20

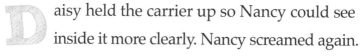

Daisy held the carrier up so Nancy could see inside it more clearly. Nancy screamed again.

"I can't bear it!" she said. "It's worse than worms, Daisy! If I dissect my own worms, will you take it away?"

Daisy smacked her hand on her forehead. She was so annoyed! Everything was going wrong, and now Nancy was having a . . . a . . . a fit of the vapors!

Minnie swept in. She took Nancy's arm and carefully led her away. They sat down in a booth

far from Daisy. Daisy watched as Minnie patted Nancy's hand and talked in a low, soothing voice.

Daisy couldn't hear what they were saying. But when Minnie came back, she was shaking her head.

"She won't help us," Minnie said. "She thinks Sugarplum wants to bite her. She also thinks Sugarplum has **rabies**. And **tetanus**. And **lice**. And a bad attitude."

Well, that part is true, Daisy thought.

"This is silly," Daisy said. "Sugarplum is annoying, sure. But he's not that scary looking!"

"Yeah," Minnie said. "**He's kind of cute.** Maybe if Nancy could see him up close, out of the carrier, she'd get over it."

Daisy decided it was worth the risk. They needed Nancy's help.

Daisy opened the door of the carrier.

Sugarplum was so fast, he was barely a blur. He launched himself into the air . . .

. . . and landed on Abigail's head! There was a sugar bowl on the shelf behind her, and Sugarplum dived for it.

"Didn't Mrs. Flamingo say he shouldn't have sugar?" Minnie said. She and Daisy stared at Sugarplum. **He was cramming sugar into his mouth.**

"Yeah," Daisy said. "But what's the worst that could happen? He's already bouncing off the walls."

"Oh no!" Minnie said. "There's a chocolate ice cream cake on the counter and he's headed right for it! Isn't chocolate on the list of no-nos, too?"

"**I am in so much trouble,**" Daisy muttered. "At this point I might as well give him a peanut butter sandwich on whole wheat bread and take him to a Justin Beakber concert. It could hardly get worse."

SUGAR

Chapter 21

"I'm not volunteering," Nancy said. "But maybe you should do some research about sugar gliders." She was standing on the other side of the shop, keeping her distance from Sugarplum.

"I tried," Daisy said. "Leonard gave me this app full of animal facts. But it's all in some weird foreign language." She looked at the app again. "It's in Helgeborgheisen, whatever that is."

"Helgeborgheisen is my native language!" Gretel said. She hurried over. "¿Sprunka die

Helgeborgheisen?" she asked Daisy.

Daisy stared at her.

"That means, '**Do you speak Helgeborgheisen?**'" Gretel explained. "I guess you don't."

"No," Daisy said. "But my animal facts app does. Can you translate it for us?"

"Agh, yeh," Gretel said. "Ik kin gesprëktanken die håmmergläuber pør bik."

Daisy stared at her.

"That means I'd be happy to translate for you," Gretel said.

"Okay," Daisy said. She pointed at the screen. "Can you read this section and translate for us?" she said. She pointed at the gobbledygook she'd shown to Minnie.

"¡Jøu tråtteldiyårisk vil an vreunþa!" Gretel said with excitement. "**Of course!**"

Chapter 22

While Daisy and Minnie were talking to Gretel, Sugarplum was creating a mess in the ice cream parlor. After finishing off the chocolate ice cream cake, he spotted a boy eating an ice cream sundae.

Sugarplum flung out his arms, leaped into the air, and flew over Minnie's and Daisy's heads.

"I guess that's why they're called sugar gliders," Daisy observed. "They glide toward any source of sugar!"

Finally, Gretel had finished reading, and

hmmm...

she translated for Daisy. "It says, 'Sugar gliders prefer to have companions to play with.'"

"**That's it?**" Daisy said.

"He wants a friend?" Minnie said.

"That's all?" Nancy said.

"That's sort of adorable," Millie said.

"Whatever," Abigail said. She crossed her arms and glared at Millie. Abigail hated it when Millie or Molly spoke without her permission.

"If that's the problem," Leonard said, "I think I can help."

"Like how you helped by downloading an app in Floogelslaggen?" Daisy snapped.

"Helgeborgheisen," Gretel said.

"Yeah, sorry about that," Leonard said. He picked up Daisy's Flipazoid and started pushing buttons on it. "But look—there are all sorts of apps for pets! And here's one for sugar gliders!"

"**You're kidding,**" Minnie said. "What's it called?"

"Sugar Glider Social," Leonard said. "It's like video chatting for sugar gliders."

"I can't believe the answer is so simple," Daisy said. "He was just lonely all along!"

Chapter 23

"So where is the little guy now?" Minnie said.

And that's when they heard a very loud, very girly scream.

Daisy looked over her shoulder and immediately began to laugh.

"After he finished eating Jordan's sundae, he spotted my banana milk shake, which was just brought to the table," Abigail said, wailing. "And he pounced!"

"**Uh-oh,**" Leonard said.

"Tell me when it's over," Nancy said from

under the table.

"Abigail," Molly said. Or was it Millie? Daisy could never remember. "**Are you okay?**"

"Come on," Daisy said. "She totally had it coming."

"**Daisy!**" Minnie exclaimed. She sounded disapproving. But she was fighting back a smile.

"I'm just saying," Daisy said. "Maybe Sugarplum is good for something after all."

Chapter 24

Things quieted down pretty quickly after that. Abigail stomped out, still dripping ice cream. And Daisy managed to scoop the tired little sugar glider into his carrier.

While Leonard set up the Sugar Glider Social app on Daisy's Flipazoid, Daisy, Minnie, Nancy, and Gretel got to work cleaning up the mess Sugarplum had made. They mopped, swept, and spritzed every surface.

"There's a sugar glider in Japan who wants to video chat with Sugarplum," Leonard said.

"Really?" Daisy said. Sugar gliders knew how to type?

"Well," Leonard said, "his owner just told me so."

That made more sense.

Soon, the ice cream parlor was clean again. Everyone ordered a treat, and they all sat down around a big table.

Daisy brought Sugarplum out of his carrier and showed him the Flipazoid. On the screen, another sugar glider peered out at Sugarplum.

"Look at that!" Minnie said. "They're friends already!"

The two animals were looking at each other in a very friendly way. Sugarplum chirped, and the other sugar glider chirped back.

"Good job, Leonard," Daisy said. "You did it.

This is the first time I've seen this little guy look happy!"

"I guess he is sort of cute," Nancy said. "For something that looks like a cross between a rat and a monkey."

"**Congratulations, Daisy,**" Minnie said. "This job is a success!"

Chapter 25

One week later, Daisy was back on a surfboard. But this time it was her own!

Daisy smiled and paddled into the water. She lay on the board, feeling the waves rock her back and forth.

Soon, a big wave was heading her way. Daisy braced herself, and popped up to stand.

This was the life!

"Wooo!" Minnie hollered from the beach. She was there with Nancy and Leonard to watch Daisy do her thing.

"Go, Daisy! Ride that wave!" Nancy yelled.

"Uh, radical?" Leonard said. He wasn't much of a beach guy.

"Wow," Minnie said. She watched as Daisy angled her board over a wave. "Daisy's getting good!"

"She's a natural," Nancy said. "She's taken to it like a duck to water."

Soon Daisy was ready for a break. She paddled back to the beach. She carried her board over to her friends and plopped herself down on the sand.

"Nice work out there, Daisy!" Minnie said. "How do you like Humuhumunukunukuapua'a?"

Daisy petted her surfboard affectionately. **"She's perfect,"** Daisy said.

"So," Nancy said, "was it worth it? All those awful jobs?"

"Yeah," Leonard asked. "Sugarplum was almost the end of you."

"Sugarplum isn't so bad," Daisy said. "In fact, I'm going to be pet-sitting for him every weekend. Mrs. Flamingo thinks it's good for him to have more friends."

"Hey," Nancy said, "there they are!" She pointed. Daisy turned and saw Mrs. Flamingo, dressed in a brightly colored sarong. She was walking toward them. There was a beach umbrella tucked under her arm. In her other hand, she held Sugarplum's carrier.

"Hello, kids," Mrs. Flamingo said. "I thought Sugarplum would enjoy a little field trip to the beach."

"Hi, Mrs. F," Daisy said. "I'm glad you came. I have a present for Sugarplum!" She rummaged around in her beach bag.

"Here they are!" Daisy handed Mrs. Flamingo a little bag. "Organic, sugar-free, nutritionally balanced sugar glider treats."

"It's better than a whole jar of sugar, anyhow," Minnie said. Daisy glared at her.

"What's that about a jar of sugar?" Mrs. Flamingo asked.

"Nothing!" Daisy, Minnie, Leonard, and Nancy all said together.